STAGE
School

BETHANY'S SONG

Holly Sleet

BLOOMSBURY

First published in Great Britain in 2007 by Bloomsbury Publishing Plc
36 Soho Square, London, W1D 3QY

Text copyright © Holly Skeet 2007
Illustrations copyright © Luella Jane Wright 2007
The moral rights of the author and illustrator have been asserted

A CIP catalogue record of this book is available from the British Library

ISBN 978 0 7475 8721 7

All papers used by Bloomsbury Publishing are natural, recyclable products made from
wood grown in well-managed forests. The manufacturing processes conform to the
environmental regulations of the country of origin.

Typeset by Dorchester Typesetting Group Ltd
Printed in Great Britain by Clays Ltd, St Ives Plc

1 3 5 7 9 10 8 6 4 2

www.bloomsbury.com

For all my family

Chapter One

A NIGHTMARE JOURNEY

Bethany Cheung leaned against the bus window and closed her eyes. Just for a minute. She'd had to get up at six, and she hadn't had time for breakfast — too much history homework that she should have done the night before. Her big sister Addie had shoved a piece of toast into her hand as she dashed out of the door to catch the bus, but Addie loved peanut butter and she could never remember that it

made Bethany feel sick. The toast went in the first bin Bethany saw, and she had a horrible feeling that Mr Townsend was going to say she should have done the same with her history. It just wasn't fair! With her long bus journey to school (and today was a lucky day – actually getting to sit down was a real bonus) Bethany never had time to do her homework as well as she would have liked. Mr Townsend hadn't been exactly happy with the last piece of work she'd handed in either.

She ought to be learning her French for their vocabulary test this morning, but not right now. She got the book out, and propped it open on her bag, as if that would help. A warm, dozy feeling came over Bethany as she wrapped her arms round her dance bag and snoozed.

'Excuse me? Hey?'

Oh no! Not another grumpy passenger having a go because Bethany had her bags on the seat! She opened her eyes wearily, and prepared to heave her things on to her lap.

'Sorry to wake you – you look as though you

needed that nap. But don't you normally get off here?' It wasn't a someone spitting fire at all, it was the girl with the purple hair and twenty or so earrings, who always caught this bus with Bethany. She was looking worriedly out of the window. 'This is your stop, isn't it?' she asked apologetically.

Bethany was sure the girl must have made a mistake – she'd only closed her eyes thirty seconds ago! But she checked out of the window just in case. Eek! She was right. And the bus was just starting to pull away from the kerb. 'Stop!' she yelped, grabbing the bell and ringing it about six times. 'Thank you!' she gasped to the purple-haired girl, scrambling for her stuff.

Bethany hurtled down the gangway to the doors. Unfortunately it was the grouchy driver today, and he was making a big fuss about opening them again.

'It's kids like you who make the buses run late,' he was muttering. 'Wake up, can't you?'

'Sorry.' Bethany tried hard to look as though she really was, but it was difficult. This was the guy who insisted on examining her pass each morning as

though she were a master criminal, not an eleven-year-old he saw every day. And the bus was always late anyway! At last the doors opened, and Bethany jumped out, waving gratefully at the purple-haired girl as the bus drove off.

She dumped her bags on the pavement and gave a deep sigh of relief. Thank goodness that girl had woken her up. She'd probably have ended up on the other side of London otherwise. Sleepily she slung her rucksack on to her shoulder, and grabbed her bag of dance clothes. Then she had a horrible thought. Her French textbook! 'Please, please, please let me have put it back in my bag,' she muttered to herself. But even as she scrabbled frantically through her rucksack she knew she hadn't. It was probably down the side of the seat somewhere. Ms LeBrun was going to *kill* her.

Bethany trudged tiredly up the road to school. So far, it was definitely *not* a good day. For once even the sight of the school buildings, with *The Marcia Lane School of Drama and Dance* in big gold letters above the door, failed to cheer her up. She actually

felt jealous of Addie, lounging at home watching breakfast TV until ten minutes before registration at Downsbrook, just five minutes round the corner from their flat. Bethany was shattered, and the day hadn't even started. Was it really worth all this effort just to *get* to school?

Stupid question, Bethany told herself firmly. Of course it is. You're just having a bad day. A bad week, something grumbled back. And unfortunately it was true. Bethany felt like she'd been running to catch up with herself ever since she'd discovered on Monday that their science projects were supposed to be finished – and hers had been on her bed at home, half done. So now she was on the wrong side of Mrs Taylor (which was impressive, as their science teacher was more like a fluffy teddy bear than anything else), she was about to give in some history that she'd spent all of twenty minutes on, and she had to tell their very un-teddy-bear-like French teacher that her textbook was on a bus, probably somewhere round King's Cross by now. It wasn't going to help that Ms LeBrun had caught her having

11

a little catnap in French on Friday. Lily and Chloe had done their best to nudge her awake, but they hadn't been in time to save her. And now she hadn't even revised for the test. Bethany sped up. She needed to get into school and borrow a book off one of the others, fast.

She pounded up the stairs to the Year Seven form room. Lane's school buildings were a couple of old London houses which had been converted – it couldn't be more different from Addie's purpose-built, sensibly laid-out school. It was like an intelligence test for new students just trying to work out how to get to classes. But after nearly half a term, Bethany and her mates couldn't imagine not knowing where everything was – or most places, anyway.

Bethany raced into their classroom, and thankfully found her friend Sara – with a French book. 'Can I look too?' she gasped. French was first period, and they didn't have much time. 'Course,' said Sara, sounding surprised. 'Where's yours? Left it at home?'

Bethany shook her head. 'On the bus. It's been one of those mornings.'

Sara nodded sympathetically. She caught the train to get to school, but her journey was a lot quicker than Bethany's. She'd seen how stressed Bethany got with her nightmare commute.

'Did you fall asleep again?'

Bethany nodded, running a finger down the vocab list to hide her embarrassment.

'I don't know how you manage that trip twice a day, it must be a nightmare.' Sara shuddered. 'I mean, my train's a real pain, but at least it's quick. I suppose it's all worth it though, isn't it?' she added happily.

It was the same question Bethany had asked herself only a few minutes before, but this time she didn't hesitate. Finding Sara had calmed her down a bit — she was one of Bethany's best friends. Nightmare morning though it had been, this was definitely where she wanted to be. 'Of course it is. OK, so sometimes I wish I was like my sister, just popping round the corner to school, but her school is *really* boring. And that's where I would have gone if I hadn't got in here.'

13

And if I hadn't won that scholarship, she added to herself silently.

Fees at Lane's were hugely expensive – because it cost loads to pay all the different dance, drama and singing teachers, let alone the academic staff. There was no way that Bethany's mum, managing on her own since Bethany and Addie's dad had left, could have paid the fees. It was difficult enough paying for Addie's guitar lessons and Bethany's ballet and tap as it was.

Bethany had always dreamed of going to a school like Lane's. She and Addie were both very musical – her sister sang and played guitar in a band at school – and Bethany really wanted to be a singer when she was older. Loads of her favourite stars had been to places like Lane's, and she knew it would be a fantastic opportunity. But she also knew that there was no way they could afford it. She hadn't even dared to hope for a miracle, she'd just assumed she'd be going to Downsbrook like Addie. At least they had a great music and drama department, and even a

purpose-built studio theatre. Addie loved it.

Then Miss Collins, the visiting music teacher at Bethany's primary school, who'd been giving her extra singing lessons, suggested Lane's to her mum. She didn't want to get Bethany's hopes up, but they did award scholarships for students who really excelled, so . . .

It took a week for Mrs Cheung to decide whether she should even mention it. After all, what if Bethany got really excited about it, and then didn't get in? She would be gutted. Or worse, what if she got a place, but not a scholarship? Then she'd know that she was good enough to go, and it was all down to money that she couldn't. But Mrs Cheung decided in the end that she just couldn't let Bethany miss out on this chance. On the Saturday afternoon, when Addie was out shopping with her friends, she went into their room, where Bethany was lying on her bed, reading one of Addie's magazines and listening to the MP3 player that had been her birthday and Christmas presents combined. She sat down on the bed next to her, and pulled out one of Bethany's

earphones. She normally listened to the same kind of music as the girls, and she listened along for a bit, nodding to herself.

'Bethany, can we talk for a minute?' she asked eventually, when she felt she couldn't put it off any longer.

'Mm-hm.' Bethany turned off the MP3 player, and looked questioningly at her mother.

'You know we had that parents' evening at school last week?'

'Yeah. You said it was OK! You said Mrs Thomas was really pleased with me,' Bethany asked worriedly.

'She was, love, she was. Very pleased. I was talk-ing to that Miss Collins though, about your singing. And she had a – a suggestion.'

Bethany just looked at her curiously.

Mrs Cheung twisted her fingers together. 'She thinks you should audition for a stage school.'

Bethany sat up straighter. 'Wow, really? Did she actually think I might get in?' Her eyes sparkled at the thought. 'I mean, I know I couldn't go, but it's

cool that she thought I was good enough, isn't it, Mum?'

Bethany's mum felt furious. It was so unfair that Bethany should be ten years old and already have given up on her dream, just because of money. She was too young to have to think like that. She swallowed. 'She thinks there's maybe a chance that you could go,' she said cautiously. 'Just a chance, mind.'

Bethany shook her head. 'No way, Mum. Addie and I looked on the net. Have you seen how much those places cost? It's like thousands of pounds a *term*!'

'I know.' Bethany's mum didn't mention that she'd spent ages looking at those same websites, sadly scribbling sums on little scraps of paper. Bethany was right. There was no way. Unless . . .

'Miss Collins reckons you could maybe apply for a scholarship. They have them, apparently, at these places. They'd cover the fees, and give you something towards your uniform. We'd just have to find the money to get you there. She suggested the Marcia Lane School – she said she's got some friends

17

who teach there, and it's very good.'

Bethany was gazing at her like she'd suggested a trip to Disneyworld. 'That was one of the websites we looked at, Mum!' she breathed. 'It's one of the best schools in the country. Jasmine Day went there!' She waved the MP3 player at her mum – they'd been listening to Jasmine's debut album.

'Bethany, listen. It *is* one of the best schools in the country, and it's impossibly hard to get into. It's going to be even harder to get a scholarship. And I'm sorry, love, but it's like you say – the fees are huge. Without the scholarship we couldn't do it. So it's probably a thousand to one chance.' She shrugged helplessly at her daughter. 'Do you want to try?'

Of course Bethany did. She totally understood everything her mum said about it being really unlikely she'd get in *and* get a scholarship, but she had to *try*, didn't she?

And the thousand to one chance had worked. Bethany thought it was probably because she'd been quite relaxed at the audition – it had all seemed so

unlikely she hadn't really got too keyed up about it. Now that she was here, it was better than she could ever have imagined – dance, theatre and music classes every afternoon, with brilliant teachers. It was just the travelling that was such a nightmare. Still, she had no right to moan. Loads of the students made crazy journeys to get to Lane's. She was by no means the only one.

'Of course it's worth it,' she told Sara, in a voice that was almost naturally cheerful. 'I could do without grumpy bus drivers, that's all. And grumpy French teachers. Ms LeBrun's going to kill me.'

Sara really wanted to say something encouraging, but she had to settle for 'Mmmm'. Their French teacher was OK, but she wasn't known for her patience. 'Perhaps if you do really well in this test you could tell her about your book afterwards,' she went on hopefully.

'Ye-es,' Bethany agreed. 'Course, there's one snag with that.'

'Mmm, but you're quite good at French normally. Here, have the book.' And Sara thrust the book at

Bethany, grinning. 'I reckon I've learned it enough. I wouldn't like to give Ms LeBrun a heart attack by getting too many right.'

'There they are!' Lily and Chloe raced into the classroom, both grinning, and hurtled to a stop by Sara and Bethany.

'We did it!' Chloe squeaked, dancing up and down. 'We got the parts in *Little Women*, both of us. Can you believe it?'

'That's brilliant!' Sara gasped. 'The parts you wanted?'

Lily nodded. 'Yes, I'm going to be Beth and Chloe's got Amy. It's just perfect!'

Bethany hugged them both quickly. 'That's so exciting! Well done! I can't believe you're going to be on TV!' She couldn't help feeling a tiny hint of jealousy – she wished *she* had had an audition, but so far she hadn't even been considered for anything. There was no way she wanted Lily and Chloe to see that though – she really was pleased for them as well.

Chloe looked like she couldn't stand still for excitement. 'We're going to be staa-aars!' she sang,

twirling around, her curly red hair flying round her head.

'You're going to have to calm down sometime, Chloe! I bet you didn't sleep at all!' Sara giggled. 'Hey, why didn't you call us?'

Lily and Chloe exchanged embarrassed glances. 'We-ell,' Lily explained slowly. 'I didn't know if Chloe had got a part, and she didn't know if I had –'

'I did ask Ms Shaw, but she wouldn't tell me,' Chloe put in.

'So we both kind of wanted to wait until we'd found that out before we told you. I mean, I don't think I'd have felt the same way about it if Chloe hadn't got a part too.'

Chloe shook her head. 'And it seemed a bit weird to ring up and ask Lily, so I was waiting until this morning. Then we saw each other in the entrance hall and it was totally obvious!'

'I don't think I've stopped grinning since Ms Shaw phoned last night,' Lily agreed.

'What did your mum say?' Bethany asked gently. Lily had been under real pressure from her mum.

21

She was an actress, and she'd been desperate for Lily to act too – whatever it took.

Lily smiled, and Bethany thought she hadn't seen her look so relaxed and happy in ages. 'That's the best part! I had this really good talk with my mum after the audition. She's promised to stop trying to run my life for me!'

'So, is she going to back off?' Sara asked.

Lily nodded enthusiastically. 'She said she'll still help with whatever I want, but I have to ask her. She's keeping well out of it. And you know what, now she's said that, I think I probably will ask her to help me with learning my scenes – she does have really good ideas.'

'Hey, do you think she'd coach me too?' Chloe asked, grinning.

Bethany shook her head in amazement. 'I totally can't believe you're talking about the same person! After what you said on Monday!'

Seeing Sara and Chloe so excited, Bethany couldn't help feeling that sharp sense of jealousy again.

Why wasn't this happening for her too?

Chapter Two

BETHANY'S TURN

Chloe and Lily's big news pretty much axed any further French revision, so Bethany wasn't feeling too confident as Ms LeBrun strode into the classroom half an hour later. It was stupid – normally she loved shopping, even though she never had much allowance to spend, so learning the names of shops should have been a doddle. She reckoned she was OK on the list of things you could buy at the

boulangerie, though. She could just do with a *pain au chocolat* right now.

Everyone sighed and shoved away their textbooks as their smartly dressed teacher beamed evilly at them. 'Are we all ready for our little vocabulary test?' she asked sweetly. She perched herself on the desk in front of them with the book, and proceeded to read out a list of words in English for them to turn into French — most of which, Bethany was ready to swear, had not been on the list they'd been told to learn. What on earth was the French for sausages?

She grimly filled in as many as she could, but she really didn't have a good feeling about this, and she cast a panicky glance at Sara. Her friend was scribbling and gazing raptly at her paper, though, her long blonde hair falling in a curtain that hid her face. Bethany quickly scanned round their table. Lily was concentrating like Sara, and Chloe — surprise, surprise — was staring into space with a happy smile on her face. As Bethany watched she suddenly caught herself in her daydream, and stared down at her test

paper. French clearly wasn't the first thing on her mind today.

Ms LeBrun got them to mark each other's tests, and Sara's face was not encouraging as she ticked — or mostly crossed, it looked like — Bethany's answers. As she totted them up she glanced apologetically at her friend. 'Only eight right. I'm sorry, Bethany.'

Eek! Eight out of twenty? Ms LeBrun was going to love that.

'I only got nine,' Chloe said encouragingly. 'It was a really hard test. Don't worry about it.'

Mmmm. That was all very well for Chloe to say, but she wasn't at Lane's on a scholarship — one that was 'conditional upon performance'. Which meant that Bethany had to do really well not just at the drama and dance classes, but academic work too. And after her disastrous performance in science, history and now French this week, no one was going to say she was managing that. Bethany chewed the end of her long black plait miserably. Just how useless did you have to be to get thrown out of stage

school? Or have your scholarship taken away? Because for her, it would be the same thing.

It wasn't even as if she'd been doing so well in her stage classes that they'd overlook the poor classwork, she worried to herself. Sara had her part in *Mary Poppins*, and now Chloe and Lily had done brilliantly in the auditions for a major drama series. No one had even mentioned Bethany auditioning for anything. If things carried on like this, maybe the school was going to start thinking the scholarship should have gone to somebody else.

Luckily, Bethany wasn't the only one who'd done badly on the test – Chloe's mate Sam came bottom with four out of twenty. But she did get a particularly unimpressed glare from Ms LeBrun when she told the teacher her mark. She supposed she couldn't expect much else after dozing off in the previous lesson. Now was definitely not the time to admit she'd left her French book on the bus. So it was a bit of a disaster when Ms LeBrun saw her sharing Sara's book, and snapped, 'Bethan-ee! Your book, where is it?' She always sounded more French when she was cross.

Bethany just stared at her like a sick goldfish, wondering what on earth to say. But Sara gave Ms LeBrun her best smile.

'Actually this is Bethany's book, Ms LeBrun. I left mine in my locker, and Bethany's sharing with me. Sorry!'

Sara had pulled out all the stops and got seventeen on the vocab test, so she was in Ms LeBrun's good books. The French teacher just smiled and nodded, and carried on with the lesson.

'Thank you!' Bethany whispered, as soon as Ms LeBrun wasn't looking.

'No problem.' Sara grinned. 'I think she might have bitten your head off otherwise!'

Bethany managed to survive the rest of the morning without any more comments on her work. They had science, but she'd handed in her project the day before with a grovelling note, and Mrs Taylor seemed to be OK about it. She was still feeling a bit down at lunchtime. She picked at her salad while the others eagerly discussed the *Little Women* auditions.

Sara nudged her. 'Hey, are you OK?' she asked quietly, as Chloe and Lily argued about what Ms Shaw, the school's agent, had said would happen next.

Bethany shrugged. 'Just worrying about that book. I can't keep "lending" it to you!'

Sara grimaced. 'Maybe Ms LeBrun will have calmed down by next lesson,' she said hopefully.

'It's *possible*,' said Bethany thoughtfully. Then they looked at each other and started giggling. 'Calm' and 'Ms LeBrun' just didn't really go together all that well. Still, Bethany felt a bit better. They had singing that afternoon – her favourite class. Even though Mr Harvey was as mad as a weasel on his worst days, he was still a brilliant teacher, and Bethany knew that her voice was improving all the time in his classes.

Today Mr Harvey seemed to be even crazier than usual. There was a kind of suppressed excitement about him, and his warm-up exercises went one step beyond weird. 'Chocolate!' he announced dramatically as he sat down at the piano. Everyone looked

hopeful. 'A brilliant word for working the facial muscles. Chocolate, chocolate, chocolate, chocolate, chocolate!' he sang up the scale to demonstrate, making elaborate chewing motions as he went. 'Everybody! Work those mouths!'

Everyone obediently chewed away on their imaginary chocolate – as well as they could for laughing. But he was right, it really did seem to loosen up their mouth muscles, which was good as Mr Harvey was always yelling in the middle of songs that no one in the class opened their mouths wide enough.

After nearly an hour of picking a song to pieces, Mr Harvey crashed down the piano lid. Everyone jumped, but for once this didn't seem to be because he was about to have a rant. He grinned round at them all, and Bethany decided excitedly that he was finally about to tell them why he was looking like a cat that had got a whole fridgeful of cream.

'I have good news for some of you,' he purred, standing up and leaning on the piano top. 'Who's heard about the Wish concert at the Albert Hall next month?'

'That big charity concert, sir?' someone piped up from the back.

'Exactly. "Big" being the operative word. Massive charity concert with loads of top stars, all in aid of children's charities. Well, since it's to raise money for children, they'd like some children in it. Which is where you lot come in.'

'Us?' Bethany squeaked delightedly. 'Really? Jasmine Day's singing in that concert, and loads of other brilliant people!'

'Not all of you. Just ten people from Years Seven and Eight. But you Bethany, I'm happy to say, are on my little list.' Bethany was actually jumping up and down and hugging Lily by now.

'Wow, I'm so jealous,' Lily breathed. 'Well done, Bethany!'

'Let me see. Year Sevens. Yes. Bethany, Chloe, Sam – was I out of my mind? Sam, you'd better watch yourself –'

'Sir,' Sam agreed, grinning all over his face. He was one of the class's worst jokers, but he did have a very good voice.

Mr Harvey carried on reading out names. 'Jade, Daisy and Aiden. And remember you lot, any bad reports of you, and you'll be out – this is a very prestigious event for the school to be asked to take part in. Do *not* let me down!' He was doing his superfearsome scowl now, but the six people he'd named were too excited to notice.

'Chloe!' Bethany skittered over to hug her too. 'This is so cool! We're going to be in the same concert hall with Jasmine Day!'

'Better than that, Bethany.' Mr Harvey went back to the Cheshire cat impression. 'Jasmine Day is the singer you'll actually be performing with. You'll be part of her backing group. She requested students from Lane's – you know she was a student here.'

'Did you teach her, Mr Harvey?' Chloe asked breathlessly. Bethany was speechless by now.

'Uh-huh. Never opened her mouth enough. Very lazy.' Mr Harvey sniffed disgustedly, and most of the class fell about giggling. Imagine Jasmine Day being yelled at by Mr Harvey for not opening her mouth!

31

'Nice voice though,' he admitted grudgingly, which was very high praise from him. 'Right, the bell's about to go. I'll let you know about the rehearsal schedule – mostly it's going to be after school.'

Chloe was looking worried as they strolled over to the drama studio. 'I hope the rehearsals aren't going to clash with any of the *Little Women* stuff. I don't want to miss out on either of them!'

'They probably won't,' Lily said reassuringly. 'That's only going to be one or two days, for costume fittings and that sort of thing. There's ages till the actual filming.'

Finally Bethany could listen to them discussing their parts without feeling a bit like a loser. Now that this brilliant chance had come through for her, she could actually admit that that was how she'd been thinking of herself. 'Spoilt brat,' she said to Chloe, shaking her head and grinning. 'If only we all had such problems!'

Chloe elbowed her. 'Us geniuses,' she said grinning. 'Though actually, if it hadn't been for *Mary Poppins*, there's no way he'd have chosen me – it

32

would have been you, Sara, your voice is way better. Don't you mind?'

Sara shook her head. 'Oh, maybe a tiny bit, but not really. I'm more into musicals anyway. You know the *Mary Poppins* thing is my dream part.'

Bethany shook her head. She could see that Sara really meant it, but she couldn't see *how*. A chance to sing with Jasmine Day – even only for one night – just wasn't something she could bear to miss. She floated through their acting class in a delighted haze, but her commute home had never seemed longer. She was desperate to get back and tell Addie, and Mum, who'd be home from her job at the hair salon soon after Bethany got there.

Addie was curled up on the sofa with yet more toast and peanut butter – ugh – and a magazine. She looked up in surprise as Bethany hurtled into the flat. This whirlwind clearly had news. Bethany threw herself down on the sofa next to her sister. 'I thought so,' she said joyfully, grabbing Addie's magazine.

'Hey!' squawked Addie, nearly losing her toast as she tried to grab *Sugar* back.

But Bethany wasn't listening. 'Look!' She stabbed her finger at the very feature Addie had been dripping peanut butter on. There was a big photo of Jasmine Day, grinning into the camera and wearing a Wish T-shirt – although it looked like it had been spray-painted on to her. 'I thought I'd read something about it. You see this – about the big charity concert she's singing in? I'm singing in it too! Ten of us from school are going to be her backing group!'

'No way!' said Addie suspiciously. 'You are kidding, aren't you?'

'Uh-uh! I swear to you, we found out in singing today.' Bethany read the article again eagerly, hoping to find out some interesting details. Mr Harvey had been irritatingly short on the more gossipy side of things. But it was mostly about how Jasmine Day had been really excited to be appearing in the concert, because she'd suffered similar problems to some of the children Wish was trying to help. 'Wow, I wonder what,' Bethany murmured, pointing this out to Addie.

Addie was still trying to get her head round her little sister singing at the Albert Hall. So far she hadn't really felt jealous of Bethany going to Lane's – she liked her own school, and Lane's sounded too much like hard work – but singing with Jasmine Day? That was amazing.

'I can't believe it,' she said, grabbing the magazine back again. 'You're really going to be in this? Wait till I tell everyone at school! Isn't it going to be on TV?'

'I think so,' Bethany agreed happily. 'I can't wait to tell Mum!' On cue there was the sound of a key in the front door.

Mrs Cheung was slightly surprised to be met at the door by both her daughters waving a magazine and shrieking. It took a while for her to work out what was going on, but then she decided they had to celebrate with pizza and a DVD.

It was a bit of a downer for Bethany to have to get up at six again the next morning, and scramble through the homework she hadn't managed to fit in

the night before – which was most of it, although she hadn't let Mum know that. But as she stood yawning at the bus stop, Bethany just had to think 'concert' for it all to be worthwhile. Unfortunately there was nowhere to sit on the bus, so she clung on to the rail and daydreamed.

'Hey!' It was the purple-haired girl from yesterday again. Bethany looked round in a panic. Surely she hadn't missed her stop? She *couldn't* have gone to sleep standing up, could she?

The older girl giggled. 'No, it's OK! You've got ages. You really were away with the fairies. Anyway, I've got something for you.' She rummaged around in a cool straw bag covered in flowers. 'Got it here somewhere.' At last she triumphantly brought out a book. 'You left it yesterday when you had to get off in such a hurry.'

'My French book! You star!' Bethany felt like hugging her. 'Thank you!' It seemed like suddenly everything was going to be all right!

'Not a problem. Do you go to some kind of special school? I can't believe you do this journey

every day – it's bad enough me doing it to get to uni.'

Bethany nodded happily. 'I go to a stage school,' she explained. 'Lane's, in Bloomsbury.'

'I can see why you make the effort then!' The older girl looked impressed. 'Wow. Would I have seen you in anything?'

Bethany blushed. This felt so cool! 'No, not yet. But I'm going to be in a big charity concert soon. The Wish concert at the Albert Hall? We're singing with Jasmine Day.'

The girl with purple hair looked very impressed. 'How do you fit that kind of thing in with school-work, though?' she asked interestedly. 'I mean, you can't have much time at home as it is.'

Bethany just stared at her. This wasn't even something she'd considered, although now, after the disasters of yesterday morning, she wondered how she could have been so stupid. How on earth was she going to fit in the rehearsals, and her homework, and the travelling? She never got home much before five-thirty now, and Mr Harvey had said the Wish

rehearsals would be after school. Homework wasn't going to get a look-in! And there were hardly any buses home later in the evening. Bethany looked stricken, and the older girl looked back worriedly. 'Hey, sorry, did I say something wrong? I was just wondering.'

'No, no, it's OK,' Bethany stammered. 'I just hadn't really thought about it much yet. That kind of thing, I mean. We only found out we were in it yesterday.'

'I'm sure it'll be OK. Who cares about homework anyway?' And the girl grinned at her.

Bethany tried to smile back as though she agreed, but she knew she didn't have a choice. She *had* to care about homework, however much she didn't want to. And she couldn't help worrying about all the trouble she'd had with work lately. It was awful even to think about it — but maybe she couldn't be in the concert after all?

Chapter Three

LEAVING HOME

Bethany hurried off the bus and headed into school. The worst thing was, she couldn't even discuss this with Chloe, Lily and Sara. Or not without hiding what was really bothering her, anyway. She'd decided ages ago that she wasn't going to tell anyone else about her scholarship. She just wasn't sure how people would react – and she didn't really like the idea of everyone knowing her mum couldn't afford

to pay the school's fees. She knew that Sara's gran paid half of hers, but she got the impression that that was more because Sara's parents didn't really want to be shelling out for a school they disapproved of than because they couldn't afford it. Sara's gran had been a professional dancer, and she was delighted that her granddaughter had won a place at Lane's. Chloe and Lily's parents obviously had no trouble paying for them. Bethany was pretty sure Lane's only gave one scholarship a year, so obviously everyone else in her class had parents who could pay the fees. Bethany really didn't want to be the odd one out.

What on earth was she going to do? Bethany seriously couldn't imagine going to find Mr Harvey and telling him she couldn't do the concert after all. She'd probably be able to make him understand eventually, but he'd go ballistic first. She shuddered. No, she needed to find someone sympathetic to talk to – someone on the staff, who must all already know about her scholarship. She trudged through the hall, looking miserable and wondering who she

could ask. She was staring at the floor, so she didn't notice Miss Jasper, their ballet teacher, coming the other way – until she walked into her.

'Ooops!' Luckily Miss Jasper was really nice, and she just put out her hands to catch Bethany's shoulders and steady her. 'Watch out, Bethany! Are you OK?' she added, looking at Bethany's eyes, which were red-rimmed from trying not to cry. Knowing that she was in the concert with Jasmine Day had been like a dream come true for all of eighteen hours, but ever since the girl on the bus had made her realise that she couldn't be in the concert Bethany had felt like howling. She didn't want anyone to see her being upset though – to think she was a baby.

Bethany sniffed. Miss Jasper was being *too* nice, and that was fatal. A large tear dripped down the side of her nose, even as she nodded brightly. 'I'm fine,' she muttered. Then a thought struck her. Miss Jasper wasn't actually anything to do with the concert, of course, but maybe she could give her some advice, maybe even talk to Mr Harvey for her. But

actually telling someone she was giving up the chance of a lifetime was too much. She just couldn't. Bethany made a strange gulping noise and looked round for somewhere to run.

Miss Jasper was still holding her. She steered Bethany into an empty office off the hallway, and pushed her into a chair. 'Talk to me,' she said firmly. She could see that comforting Bethany was just going to make her worse. 'What is it?' Her brisk voice calmed Bethany down, and she managed to hold back any more tears. She explained as quickly as she could, feeling really embarrassed as she mentioned the scholarship and her problems with work. Luckily Miss Jasper didn't seem to care very much about that.

'I see,' she said thoughtfully. 'Mmm. We obviously need to do something, but I don't think giving up the concert is the answer, Bethany. After all, that's what you're here for, isn't it?'

'You don't think so?' Bethany looked up at her in sudden hope. Then she sighed. 'But I just don't see how I can fit the rehearsals in. There *isn't* anything else I can do.'

'Of course there is!' The ballet teacher shook her head, smiling. 'Bethany, we have this kind of problem all the time! Loads of the students come from a long distance. A couple of girls in Year Nine even moved down to live with relatives when they got their places. They go home at weekends. And that's the kind of thing I'm thinking we could arrange for you – just for the rehearsal period for the concert. If you were living closer to school, you'd be able to fit everything in. What do you think?'

Bethany nodded slowly. It seemed like the perfect answer. 'But . . . where would I live?' she asked, a little anxiously.

'Well, the school has a sort of boarding house a couple of streets away. Some of the older students doing diplomas stay there,' Miss Jasper explained. 'I should think they can fit you in for a couple of weeks. It quite often gets used for that kind of thing. I'll talk to your form tutor about it, and she can get in touch with your mum. OK?'

Bethany nodded, feeling a little dazed. The idea of not living at home was pretty scary, but at the

moment most of her mind was full up with *I can do the concert after all!*

'Hey, Bethany!' Someone bounced up in front of Bethany as she walked slowly out of the office. 'What were you talking to Miss Jasper about?' It was Chloe, looking even bubblier than usual. Excitement about the concert was practically oozing out of her.

'We were trying to work out how I can still do the concert,' Bethany started to explain, but Chloe interrupted, looking suddenly horrified.

'*Still* do it? What do you mean? Why shouldn't you be able to do it? What's happened?'

Bethany giggled at her panicked face – it was nice that somebody else really wanted her to be there! 'Calm down! It's just that I realised on the bus this morning that it's going to be really hard to do after-school rehearsals, and get home afterwards and fit in homework and everything.'

Chloe looked doubtful. Homework was definitely not her top priority, and she was a bit surprised that Bethany seemed so worried about it.

44

'I've already been in loads of trouble this week,' Bethany explained. 'I'm just scared they might take me out of the concert group if they think I can't cope.' It was almost the truth . . .

Chloe nodded. *That* she could understand. 'That would be awful,' she murmured. 'So, did Miss Jasper say anything that might help?'

'Yeah – she reckons I might be able to go and stay in a student house round the corner until the concert. She's going to get Miss James to call my mum. My sister'll be over the moon getting our bedroom all to herself.'

Chloe looked amazed. 'Wouldn't you mind, being away from home?' she asked curiously. 'I don't think I'd like it. When I did filming before, they always arranged it so my mum came too – I was only nine, so I think they had to.'

Bethany shrugged. 'Well, it'll be a bit weird, I suppose. But it might be fun. Anyway, loads of people our age go to boarding school, don't they? It'll only be like that. I just hope my mum says I can.'

The bell went then, and they had to tear off to

registration in a hurry, and Bethany shared her news with Lily and Sara. Sara was almost jealous – although her mum was resigned to her being at Lane's now, she still didn't really approve, and she kept a watchful eye on Sara's homework.

'She's always checking to make sure we're being taught to the same standard as at her stupid school,' Sara grumbled. 'But I think we must be – she was looking at my science book last week and she looked really disappointed.' She grinned to herself. 'I'll have to tell my gran about you going to stay in digs, Bethany. She was always staying in boarding houses when she was a dancer. She said you never knew what they'd be like, some of them were lovely, but lots of them had horrible old ladies in charge who measured how much bathwater you used!'

Lily nodded. Her mum often had good show business stories. 'Yes, my mum said she stayed somewhere once and they had the same porridge reheated at breakfast time every day for a week. They all lived on sandwiches for that play, and gave their food to the cat.'

'It's very grown-up, staying on your own,' Sara added. 'Do you think your mum will be OK with it?'

'It's not really on my own,' Bethany explained. 'There's a sort of housemother who looks after everybody, and Miss Jasper said she wouldn't be surprised if other people from the concert group had to stay too. No one from our year will, though, will they? Jade and Daisy and Aiden don't come in from that far, I think. Where does Sam live?'

'Actually, I think he does have to do a horrible journey, he was moaning about his trains being late all last week,' Chloe said thoughtfully.

'Hmm, I'm not sure I'd want to share a house with Sam,' said Sara, wrinkling her nose. 'You never know when you might find a spider in your bag, or something.'

Bethany nodded. 'I know what you mean. But it would be nice to know somebody. I still don't know who the other four people in the group are. Did Mr Harvey say they were Year Eight?'

Sara nodded. 'I think so. It might be Amy and Izzy, who did the audition for *Mary Poppins* with me

– they've got good voices. They were really nice. If I see Nathan around today, I'll ask him.' Nathan was playing Michael Banks, Sara's brother in *Mary Poppins*.

Chloe giggled. 'What are the chances of you *not* seeing him? He pops up everywhere, Sara! I swear he's got the cafeteria staked out waiting for you to arrive, so he can accidentally-on-purpose come and sit with us.'

Sara blushed. 'That's not true,' she protested, but she didn't sound very convinced. 'I'm just not sure what's going on with that,' she admitted. 'Sometimes I think he *might* be interested, but he probably only wants to talk about the show, that's all.' She went even redder as the other three crowed with laughter.

'He's so going to ask you out,' Bethany said firmly. 'He's probably just worried you'll say no, and then it'll be really difficult working with you.'

Chloe nodded wisely. 'It's your duty to put the poor thing out of his misery,' she agreed.

❋ ❋ ❋

Miss Jasper had obviously worked fast, as Miss James seemed to be totally clued up on the situation when she came to do the register. 'I'll give your mum a call at break, Bethany, and see what she thinks,' she said, making a note to herself.

'Thanks, Miss James.' Bethany shook her head slightly. It was all going so fast! How did she really feel about staying away from home? She had hardly done it before, except for a school trip in her last year at primary school, and that was only a weekend. She supposed she would just have to see what it was like, but at the moment she felt more excited than nervous, which had to be a good sign.

Miss James popped into their form room at break to say that she'd spoken to Bethany's mum, who was fine about her staying in the school house. She would stay Monday, Tuesday, Wednesday and Thursday nights, and go home on Fridays. That would fit in with the rehearsals too, although there might be a couple the weekend before the concert that she'd have to come in specially for. Bethany just nodded. Wow. It was a good thing she *wasn't*

nervous about staying away. She was pretty sure her mum would miss her, though. She wondered if Miss James had had to persuade her at all – Addie and Bethany were very close to their mum, especially now it was only the three of them. Still, it was only for a couple of weeks – and then she, Bethany Cheung, was going to be on stage with Jasmine Day!

Sara clicked her fingers under Bethany's nose, laughing. 'Snap out of it, Bethany! We've got to get to history. Were you planning wild midnight parties in your new house?'

Bethany shook her head. 'No, just thinking about the concert.' She looked at Sara thoughtfully. Would her friend understand if she explained a bit about how she'd been feeling? Chloe and Lily were off getting their books from their lockers, so it was a chance to talk to Sara alone. 'I'm really glad I'm getting to be in it,' she explained, and then realised that Sara was giving her a 'Well, yeah!' kind of look. 'I mean because all of the rest of you have done so well getting parts – I was feeling a bit useless.'

'Oh! You muppet!' Sara gave her a hug. 'I know

what you mean, 'cause I'd have felt the same if it was me, but it's all just luck, isn't it? But you know you've got a brilliant voice. This concert's just going to be the start, I bet.'

Sara's prediction didn't help Bethany's daydreaming. Or rather, it did, too much. Which was a bit dangerous, as Mr Townsend hadn't been impressed with the class's history homework – the piece Bethany had spent all of twenty minutes on, and got a C for – and he was not in a patient mood. Bethany had to make a real effort to concentrate through their double period, and she was glad to get to lunch.

'Oooh, look who's here,' Chloe sniggered into her orange juice. 'There's a surprise, Sara!'

Nathan was strolling past, trying to look as though he hadn't noticed them.

'Oh, but that's good!' Sara waved at him, and he hurried over eagerly. 'We can ask him if he knows who else is in your backing group.'

Nathan squashed himself on the end of the table, as close to Sara as he could, despite Chloe cruelly

telling him there was loads of space by her.

He nodded when Bethany asked about the concert. 'Yeah, there's four people from our year. Amy, you remember her, Sara? And a mate of mine called Ethan, he's cool. And, er . . .' He trailed off, just as someone tapped Bethany on the shoulder. She'd been listening intently, as she knew a few of the Year Eights by sight and she was wondering if it would be someone who seemed nice, so she jumped.

Lizabeth, the stunning blonde Year Eight girl who'd tried to trick Sara out of her *Mary Poppins* audition, was standing behind her.

'. . . and Lizabeth and Nadia,' Nathan finished, shrugging apologetically.

'Guess what, Bethany?' Lizabeth cooed sweetly. 'Looks like you and me are sharing a room for the next two weeks. It's going to be *such* fun!'

Chapter Four

LIVING WITH THE ENEMY

It was a bombshell. The news that Lizabeth was staying in the school house too almost (but not quite) destroyed Bethany's excitement about the concert. How *did* Lizabeth do it? Bethany supposed it was because she was so pretty – and admittedly, she did have a lovely singing voice, with a crystal-clear tone to it.

'I didn't know she lived out of London,' Lily said in horror.

Bethany was still too thunderstruck to say anything. She was just watching Lizabeth stalk triumphantly out of the cafeteria, Nadia and the rest of her little gang trailing after her.

'We wouldn't, would we?' Sara muttered. 'Oh, Bethany! I'm really sorry! Are you going to be OK with this?'

'Perhaps you could tell Miss James you'd rather stay at home after all?' Chloe suggested. 'I mean, keeping up with your homework – it's not that vital, is it? Not if it means two weeks of living with Lizabeth.'

Bethany gritted her teeth, and then smiled – a slightly scary combination. It made her look like a fierce little lapdog. 'It can't be that bad, can it?' she said firmly. 'I mean, what can she *do*?'

The others were looking doubtful, especially Nathan, who'd had more experience of Lizabeth, being in her year. 'You'd be surprised,' he muttered darkly.

But Bethany knew she didn't have a choice. She wouldn't be able to keep her place in the concert

group if her work slipped any more, she was sure. She would just have to cope with Lizabeth. It wasn't as if she could do anything that bad – was it?

When Bethany's mum got home, Bethany just didn't know what to say to her. She was pretty sure that her mum would be worried about the idea of her being away from home, and she didn't want to put her off any more – she couldn't bear to miss out on the concert. But how could she be enthusiastic when it meant sharing a room with Lizabeth? She'd tried talking to Addie about it, but her sister wasn't very helpful. Normally Bethany didn't care what people said about her, so Addie couldn't get her head round Bethany being scared of Lizabeth. She thought it was just silly nerves. And she was *very* happy about getting Bethany own room for a fortnight.

Bethany's mum seemed to be most worried about getting Bethany all packed over the weekend. Apparently it would be a total disaster if Bethany didn't go away with her entire wardrobe washed and ironed, and about six sets of everything spare. On

Sunday Bethany got the feeling she was lucky not to be sitting on the sofa wrapped in a towel while Mum shoved everything she owned into the machine. 'I'm mostly only going to need my uniform, Mum!' she protested. 'I'm only taking one extra bag, you know. Where do you think I'm putting that lot?'

'You never know,' her mother muttered, frantically folding.

Bethany got the feeling that her mum was worrying about the washing so that she didn't have to worry about everything else. She went over and gave her mum a hug. 'It'll be OK, you know,' she murmured in her ear.

Scarily, even though Bethany was tiny, she was almost as tall as her mum. It made her feel very grown up, and very scared at the same time. It was so weird not to be able to spill out all her problems to her mum — to know that she couldn't even mention Lizabeth, and how mean she was — but she didn't want to make her worry any more. So she just hugged her mum tighter, instead.

✳ ✳ ✳

Bethany's commute was even madder than usual on Monday, as she was lugging the huge extra bag to take to the school boarding house with her. She hadn't managed to persuade her mum that most of the washing was completely unnecessary. Everyone else on the bus kept giving her dirty looks as they bumped into her stuff, and she felt like yelling, 'It's not my fault! Do you think I want to be dragging this lot around with me?' It just showed that she was feeling really nervous, not like herself at all. And she still had to get through a day of school before she even went to the house.

It was all made worse because she seemed to keep on passing Lizabeth in the corridors, and Lizabeth kept flicking her long blonde hair at her and grinning like a shark.

Luckily for Bethany, there was lots going on to distract her. Ms Shaw sent for Chloe and Lily at morning break to give them their scripts for *Little Women*, and the whole class spent the rest of the day poring over them at every opportunity, while Lily and Chloe gazed blissfully at their lines. Lily kept

stroking the cover of her script – whenever someone else wasn't reading it.

'You're on all of this page, and this one, wow, and this one as well.' Chloe's mate Sam was leaning over her shoulder at the lunch table, and flicking through the script. 'Lots of learning, Chloe – your favourite thing.'

Chloe grinned at him. 'I know, but it's not like learning stuff for school, is it? Lines are different. Lots more interesting. And we can practise together, Lily, which will be cool.'

Lily bounced in her chair. Bethany thought she'd never seen her look so relaxed and happy. 'I know. It's going to be brilliant. And anyway you can't talk, Sam – Mr Four-out-of-twenty. And don't you dare drop ketchup on that script!'

Sam just grinned. Clearly he couldn't care less about bad marks in French. Bethany felt like kicking him.

Chloe tugged the script back from Sam. 'Hey, let me see that bit. It's an outdoor scene. In the snow! Where are they going to find snow? That'll have to

be on location, won't it?' She beamed. 'Did we tell you some of the filming's going to be in the States?'

Everyone groaned, and Sara kicked her. 'Only about half a million times.'

Chloe grinned apologetically. 'Sorry. I'll shut up now, I promise.'

'Don't be stupid!' Bethany couldn't help feeling a tiny bit guilty. Who wouldn't be excited? 'You should be making a fuss, you deserve it.' Then she put on an evil smirk. 'Of course, if you keep going on about it, we might not let you live long enough to actually *get* to the filming . . .' She chuckled as Chloe gazed worriedly back at her, clearly trying to work out just how serious she was. 'I don't mean it, Chloe! Everyone's happy for you. Really!'

'We didn't tell you the rest of our news,' Lily said smugly. 'Guess where we're going tonight.'

'America!' Sam sniggered, and Lily and Chloe glared at him.

'You've got ketchup on your chin,' Lily told him frostily, but Sam only shrugged.

'Where then?'

'A photo shoot!' Chloe's dark blue eyes were sparkling. 'The production company want to make a really big buzz about the series, Miss Shaw said, so they want publicity photos – even before we start filming!'

'That's a bit risky,' Sam muttered worriedly, and the girls gave him confused looks. He'd managed a very convincing anxious voice. 'Well, you know, they don't want to put everybody off, Chloe.'

'OK, that's it.' Chloe flounced up, grabbed Sam's tray and smacked it down on another table, next to a group of surprised and rather haughty Year Nines. 'You're so not funny!'

'Aw, Chloe! Can't you take a joke any more?' Sam moaned. 'Now I've got to go and beg them for my lunch back! Hey! He's eating my pudding!' And he shot off to rescue his tray, leaving Chloe and the others giggling hysterically.

Miss James had told Bethany that she'd be walked over to the house at the end of school, and she swept Bethany downstairs with her after end-of-school

registration. Sara, Lily and Chloe had all given her massive goodbye hugs – Bethany was starting to feel like she'd been given a death sentence. Lizabeth was waiting, with a set of cool pink bags that Bethany would have quite liked if they hadn't been Lizabeth's.

'Have you met Lizabeth, Bethany?' Miss James asking, smiling. She clearly had no idea about Bethany and Lizabeth's past history. But then, why would she? Lizabeth's talent was for getting at people in ways that never got her noticed by teachers.

Lizabeth smiled charmingly at Miss James. 'I've auditioned with Sara,' she said, her voice sugar-sweet. 'So I've seen Bethany around.'

Bethany bristled. Right, well, if Lizabeth was going to bring *that* up, it was clear that there was no truce going on here. Lizabeth was sending her a message that it was going to be a fight from the start. They set off, Lizabeth chattering politely to Miss James, and Bethany trying hard not to look like a sulky baby trailing after them.

The house was a tall, narrow one in a smart row a

couple of streets away from the school. It had window boxes, and nice curtains, and looked quite friendly. As they climbed the front steps, a group of older students came out, all laughing and chatting, and Miss James explained that they would be from the one-year diploma course that Lane's ran for over-sixteens. She led them into a tiny office in the hallway, and a dark-haired lady on the phone waved apologetically at them. 'Won't be long!' she mouthed, rolling her eyes.

Eventually she got rid of her caller, and bounced up from behind her desk. 'Lizabeth and Bethany, yes? I'm Ms Robbins, I run the house. Let's take you up to your room. You're lucky, it's a very nice one.'

Miss James checked her watch, and said, 'I need to go, girls, so I'll see you tomorrow. Have a nice evening!'

Bethany gazed after her worriedly. She might not actually *like* maths, but suddenly Miss James was the last familiar thing she had being torn away from her. Except for Lizabeth, of course. She was all *too* familiar.

Ms Robbins went on chatting as they headed up

the stairs, explaining how the house was really full at the moment, and that they were lucky to be fitted in. She led them into a room on the first floor, and Bethany looked round delightedly. It was much bigger than the room she shared with Addie at home, and she gave a little gasp as Ms Robbins showed them the tiny en-suite bathroom in one corner. Total luxury! Lizabeth was looking round haughtily, as if she was being forced to live in a pigsty. She dumped her bags on one of the beds, and sneered at the bathroom.

Ms Robbins handed each of them a printed sheet. 'Sorry, girls, but these are the rules for younger students living in the house. We have to be quite strict – effectively we're taking the place of your parents for the next couple of weeks.'

'My parents aren't strict at all,' Lizabeth muttered, running down the list of rules disgustedly. 'We have to be back in the house by *six o'clock*?'

'Well, unless you have something else arranged,' Ms Robbins replied calmly. 'You two will be having rehearsals past then anyway, won't you?'

Bethany nodded. 'The first one's tomorrow.' And despite the awfulness of Lizabeth, she could feel little bubbles of excitement fizzing in her tummy. A rehearsal for her first professional engagement!

When Ms Robbins went back downstairs, leaving them to 'settle in', Bethany sat down on the bed Lizabeth hadn't bagged, and wondered what to do next. They would have tea in half an hour or so, and there was a common room with a TV. But she felt on edge. She hadn't quite got her head round sleeping in the same room with Lizabeth till now, when she saw how close together their beds were.

'So, do you share a room at home then?' It was Lizabeth. She was sitting cross-legged on her bed, clutching an old toy cat and gazing at Bethany in a weirdly hungry way.

'Yes,' Bethany agreed cautiously. It was crazy, but she somehow felt that it was dangerous to give Lizabeth any information at all.

'Who with?'

'My sister,' Bethany admitted reluctantly. 'Why do you want to know?'

Lizabeth shrugged and smiled. 'Just being friendly. Seeing as we're going to be together so much.'

Bethany shuddered slightly. Lizabeth being nice was scarier than Lizabeth in full demon mode. She totally understood why Sara had found it so weird when Lizabeth suddenly started being so sweet about the *Mary Poppins* audition. And *then* look what happened, she thought to herself.

'So, you live way out south of London then?' Lizabeth fished delicately. 'What do your parents do?'

'My mum's a hairdresser,' Bethany muttered. 'My dad's not around any more.' She'd only been two when her dad had left, and she didn't really remember him enough to mind – but sometimes people were funny about it. But she was really proud of her mum, coping the way she had, and there was no way she was going to let Lizabeth think anything different.

'Wow! How does your mum manage to pay for

65

you to be here? Sorry to be rude, and everything, but I wouldn't have thought a hairdresser would earn enough for the fees at Lane's.' Lizabeth was leaning forward inquisitively, her deep blue eyes fixed on Bethany's, and it felt like she was sucking the information out of her.

'She's a very good hairdresser!' Bethany snapped, getting a little of her fierceness back.

'Mmmm,' purred Lizabeth silkily. 'Lane's does scholarships. Did you know? Maybe you ought to have applied for one of those.'

Bethany shifted on the bed. Lizabeth was getting a bit too close for comfort now. Her nose was actually twitching, as if she was a dog on a scent. She *knew* she had struck gold.

'Hey! That's it, isn't it?' she cooed. 'You *do* have a scholarship! That's so cool, Bethany, I'm *really* impressed. You must have done so well at your audition.' She was beaming now, but Bethany could feel how fake the smile was. Yeah, right. Impressed by her own cleverness, more like. Bethany nibbled the end of her plait, feeling panicky. The big question

was, now Lizabeth had this information, what was she going to do with it? She looked up at the Year Eight girl, wondering what would happen next.

Lizabeth bounced up from her bed. 'We should go and get tea, don't you think? We can chat more later.' And she actually linked arms with Bethany to lead her down the stairs. It felt like holding on to a dead fish.

By bedtime, Lizabeth had obviously worked out her plan. She was clever enough to have realised, from the way that Bethany hadn't wanted to admit to having a scholarship, that she hadn't told anyone about it. Now she was making the most of this. Everything she said seemed to contain a sly little dig about money, or charity, or 'But of course you wouldn't be able to afford that . . .' in a pitying kind of way.

But the worst thing she said was just after they'd turned the lights out, and Bethany was lying there wondering if she'd ever be able to get to sleep with such a poisonous creature about two metres away from her.

'Of course, you managed ever so well picking your friends,' Lizabeth said thoughtfully, and Bethany tensed up. Where was she going with this?

'I mean, Lily's parents have got to be absolutely loaded, and I'd guess Chloe's aren't hard up either. Not so sure about Sara. But getting to be best friends with a girl whose mum's on TV every other day was very clever. They don't know, of course?' She correctly interpreted Bethany's silence. 'No, I thought not,' she said triumphantly. 'Pretty good for a scholarship girl.' She yawned sleepily, and turned over. 'Night night, Bethany.'

Chapter Five

THE LIZABETH TORTURE

Lizabeth brightened up breakfast with a chatty series of comments about how *surprised* Lily and the others would be to find out about Bethany's scholarship. She wasn't saying *when* she was planning to tell them – that wasn't her style. She was going for long drawn-out torture. And Bethany just couldn't decide what to do about it. All her instincts were screaming, 'Tell Lily and the others yourself now,

before that blonde witch does it for you!' But Lizabeth had been very clever. Even in the short time she'd had, she'd managed to make Bethany feel as though she'd done something very sly by not telling everyone about her scholarship, and then making friends with Lily, whose parents were really well off – as if the whole thing had been some cunning plan.

It wasn't true, of course. Bethany hadn't even known who Lily's mum was when she found Lily in a tearful heap on their first day – after Lizabeth herself had had a massive go at her. But Lizabeth was scarily good at setting people up, and Bethany was almost starting to feel like she *had* done it on purpose. And if *she* felt like that, what would the others think? Bethany couldn't bear the idea that her friends might think she'd been playing some horrible game the whole time – she just didn't know what to do.

She was plucking up the courage to talk to them all about it as she and Lizabeth walked into school. Lizabeth said goodbye to her almost affectionately, and headed off to the Year Eight form room, leaving

Bethany practically grinding her teeth with frustration as she climbed the stairs. How could *anyone* be so fake?

Sara jumped on her as soon as she walked in the door. 'Are you OK? What was it like? Was she a total cow to you? And why didn't you text me?'

Bethany grinned, some of the tension that had been gripping her since yesterday afternoon easing away. Sara *was* a real friend. She'd been stupid to doubt it. 'Ish, scary, yes, and sorry, I was going to, but I couldn't get away from the slime-lizard. That's my new name for her, by the way.'

'Suits her.' Sara was grinning in relief. 'I'm so glad to see you. I thought you'd be a total wreck.'

'I almost am.' Bethany took a deep breath. 'Look, I ought to tell you –'

'There they are!' A delighted screech was followed by Chloe and Lily racing up to them at top speed.

'Hey, what's happened?' Sara grabbed Chloe's arms to hold her in one place – their red-headed friend seemed to have turned into a will-o'-the-wisp suddenly, and couldn't stop twisting around.

'Look!' Lily waved a scrap of paper under their noses.

'Hold still, we can't read it,' Bethany complained. 'What is it?'

Lily handed it to her, beaming. 'It's a newspaper article. From Chloe's mum's paper, this morning.'

As Bethany and Sara bent over the newspaper, Chloe started dancing around the classroom. Then she grabbed Lily and made her waltz up and down too.

'It's all about the series. Hey, that's amazing!' Bethany forgot Lizabeth immediately.

'And have you read the best bit?' Chloe squawked. 'Skip to the end! Oh, go on, the bit in the middle's just boring stuff about the director, read the end!'

'What? Ummm, shot partly in Britain, partly in America, we knew that. Lavish production . . . Wow, that's a lot of money . . . Ashton Smith's going to be in it! No! Sara, look! Really?' Bethany scanned the short paragraph again.

'Only maybe,' Lily cautioned. 'He's not signed up for definite yet.'

'Don't be so sensible, Lily. It's really boring!' Chloe hauled her on another waltz around the room. 'We're going to America WITH THE WORLD'S CUTEST ACTOR EVER!'

Lily's phone beeped and she chuckled as she read the message. 'My mum's seen it too. She says now we just have to win a couple of BAFTAs. She's really pleased.' Lily's face was glowing.

Something jolted in Bethany's stomach. Lily's mum. Lily's rich, successful actress mum. *Lizabeth*. In the excitement of the news she'd actually forgotten about it for a second. Now was clearly not the time to have a heart-to-heart with any of her mates. She felt so angry with Lizabeth for spoiling this moment. She ought to be laughing with Lily and Chloe, begging for more exciting details, and finding out about the photo shoot, but Lizabeth's veiled threats were at the back of her mind the whole time.

It was the same all day. Everyone seemed to have seen the article, and Lily and Chloe were like school celebrities. People kept pointing them out as they passed them in the corridors. Mr Lessing, their acting

teacher, stopped the girls on the way to ballet to congratulate them. He'd been brilliant about coaching Lily and Chloe for the auditions, so they spent ages telling him about the photo shoot. It turned out he knew half the actors who were going to be in the series, and he promised to tell them some juicy gossip in their next drama class. Their excited conversation left Bethany free to see Lizabeth pattering past on her way to a tap class, smiling secretively, and giving her a tiny wave. Bethany felt sick.

Even the rehearsal for the concert wasn't as special as it should have been. Oh, it *was* special, and again Bethany almost managed to forget what was going on, but Lizabeth was there too, and however much Bethany tried to stay with Chloe and avoid her, she couldn't shut her out of her mind completely.

But it was amazing, singing Jasmine Day's lyrics – not just singing along to the radio or an MP3, but being rehearsed in how to sing the backing tracks to some of her favourite songs properly, and learning all the cool harmonies. The rehearsal was in a hired

studio, which a lot of the artists for the concert were using. Jasmine wasn't there of course – she wouldn't be until the last couple of rehearsals – but Bethany was certain she recognised a few of the other people at the rehearsal from seeing Jasmine on MTV. She and Chloe kept whispering together about it in the breaks, and Sam thought it was really funny. He wasn't a big Jasmine Day fan, unsurprisingly, and he wasn't star-struck. 'Why don't you just ask if they've been on TV backing her?' he said, grinning, and they shushed him in horror.

'I can't wait till we're actually rehearsing at the Albert Hall next week,' Chloe said dreamily as they walked out. 'It's such a brilliant place – so grand.'

Bethany nodded. 'I'm so excited – I've never even been there,' she admitted.

'Well, it's a bit of long way for you, isn't it, Bethany?' Lizabeth cooed from behind her. 'Bit of a step up.' And she sailed past, following the school chaperone who was fussing about the arrangements to get them all home.

'What's she talking about?' Sam asked Bethany.

'No idea,' Bethany answered, trying not to let her voice tremble. 'She gets weirder every day, I think.'

Sam nodded, and seemed to be satisfied, but Chloe was gazing after Lizabeth suspiciously. Bethany changed the subject quickly. 'So how come you're not having to stay up here?' she asked Sam. 'Chloe said you had a nightmare journey too.'

'They did think about it.' Sam nodded. 'But then *certain people* had already bagged the room at the house, and we worked out that if my older brother stays a bit late at work he can pick me up halfway. It's all a bit complicated though, and he reckons I really owe him. I'm going to be washing his motorbike every weekend for the rest of my life.'

Bethany had escaped that one catty comment from Lizabeth, but she knew it was only the beginning. And she was right. Lizabeth kept on niggling at her when they were together, and making cryptic remarks in front of Bethany's mates whenever she saw her at school. Luckily, no one else seemed to pick these up. Chloe and Lily were so caught up in the excitement about *Little Women* that you'd

practically have to sledgehammer them over the head with a hint before they got it. Sara was up to her neck in rehearsals for *Mary Poppins* – and trying to work out what was really going on with Nathan.

The thing was, Bethany was really glad that her secret was still safe – that was just what she'd been hoping for. But at the same time, Lizabeth was getting worse and worse. She was saying much nastier stuff now, about how Lily, Chloe and Sara would hate Bethany when they found out what she'd done, and they'd tell everyone else what a liar she was. Bethany was sure it wasn't true – any of it. Or at least, she had been . . .

But none of her friends seemed to notice how upset she was, and how she was getting quieter and quieter at school, and she was beginning to worry that maybe Lizabeth was right. The others had more important things to think about than her, it was obvious. If they didn't really care about her, then they *would* think that she'd lied to them on purpose, and they'd all hate her. Bethany was so confused. She had the added worry that staying at the school

house wasn't helping her school work much either – Lizabeth was making her so miserable she couldn't concentrate, and she'd been told off in class a couple of times.

But Bethany woke up on Friday morning feeling suddenly happy. She was going home tonight! Even Lizabeth's mean comments at breakfast didn't seem as bad as before, and Bethany felt a bit more optimistic. She was being stupid. I'll talk to the others about it today, she promised herself, and she actually managed a 'don't care' grin at Lizabeth's latest little 'joke'.

At break she found her opportunity. She wanted to talk to just one of her friends to start with – she thought it would be easier, especially as she didn't know just what she was going to say. Chloe and Lily had gone off to the cafeteria to get snacks, leaving Sara and Bethany in their classroom, flicking through a magazine. No one else was close by, and Bethany realised this was it. She took a deep breath.

'Sara?'

'Mmmm? Do you think her hair looks good like that?' Sara twisted her head round to look at the picture a different way. 'Nope. Still looks terrible. She should never have had it cut off, I don't think.' She shook her long blonde hair happily.

'Sara!' Bethany's voice was a little irritable now. When you were trying to bare your soul, it was very annoying if people didn't listen. 'I need to talk to you about something.'

'What?' Sara looked up interestedly. 'Oh, did you find out more about the concert? Did they tell you what you're going to wear yet?'

'Um, yes, they said it would be white.' Bethany was temporarily distracted from her mission. 'White and silver. It should be good, I think.'

'Mmm. It's so unfair you get to wear a cool white outfit, and I'm stuck in a pinafore dress for *Mary Poppins*. I saw the design – it's covered in bows. Seriously!'

Bethany frowned. It obviously wasn't going to be easy to get Sara to listen. She tried again. 'Anyway –'

Just then Nathan popped his head round the

classroom door, and Sara seemed to brighten when she saw him – almost invisibly she sat up straighter, and her eyes began to sparkle. Bethany just slumped next to her. What was the point? Sara wasn't interested. Maybe nobody was, she thought pathetically. Then she sighed sadly as she watched Sara blushing and talking eagerly with Nathan about something. Grow up, Bethany, she told herself. It was a stupid idea anyway. She sighed. What would she have said anyway? She'd just have to cope on her own – with whatever Lizabeth was going to dig up. Roll on the weekend . . .

Bethany felt awful going back to school on Monday – much worse after her weekend's break from the Lizabeth torture. In between being miserable, she just felt furious, partly with Lizabeth, but mostly with herself. How could she be letting another girl upset her so much? Knowing it was stupid didn't help, though. Bethany was feeling like a nervous wreck, ready to quiver into a pool of jelly the next time Lizabeth so much as looked at her. Even the

thought of their first rehearsal with Jasmine Day that Tuesday evening couldn't really cheer her up.

Still, it was amazing to see the star march into the studio, accompanied by her huge entourage. Bethany couldn't help dreaming that that would be her one day. She felt Chloe squeeze her hand in excitement. They were about two metres away from Jasmine Day!

Jasmine turned out to be really nice. She insisted on being told all of their names, and she even admired the red highlights that Bethany's mum had put in for her. Bethany glowed, until she caught a glimpse of Lizabeth looking furious – *she* was the one whose looks got admired. She glared danger-ously at Bethany, and Bethany felt her throat go dry.

In the last rehearsal she and Lizabeth and Amy had been given a complicated harmony to sing together in one of the songs. Bethany loved it – it was one of those pieces of music that just sounded so right. But now she couldn't even remember the notes. When they got to that song, 'Flight', the last one they were rehearsing, all she could see was

Lizabeth, holding her gaze like a snake, hypnotising her. She tried to sing out as she'd been taught, but her voice seemed to be stuck in her throat. The voice coach for the group frowned at her, and Bethany tried again desperately. But the notes were totally wrong, and the song ground to a halt, with everybody staring at her.

The voice coach, Matt, apologised to Jasmine. 'No idea what went wrong there,' he said, staring grimly at Bethany as though he knew *exactly* what had gone wrong.

Bethany gulped, and suddenly knew that she just couldn't do this. Not with Lizabeth right next to her, psyching her out. There was no way.

'Perhaps we need to take a break?' a sweet voice suggested. It was Jasmine, and she was smiling sympathetically at Bethany. 'I know I could do with ten minutes.'

Matt nodded. 'OK. Back here in ten, everybody.'

Bethany didn't know whether to laugh or cry. Jasmine Day had noticed her – but because she'd just totally messed up one of her most beautiful songs.

Chapter Six

CHLOE TO THE RESCUE

Chloe grabbed Bethany and shoved her out of the studio at lightning speed before Matt could have a go at her. 'What on earth's the matter?' she demanded, as they got out of the door. 'You could sing that perfectly last time. Is it just nerves 'cause Jasmine's here?' She shook her head. 'No, that's not like you. Come on, tell me!'

She hustled Bethany to a sofa by the drinks

machine, and stared at her, in the same information-sucking way that Lizabeth had. Somehow Chloe's glare was so different, though.

'Hey.' A soft voice sounded behind them, and both girls jumped. It was Jasmine, for once unaccompanied by her string of minders. Chloe looked around disbelievingly.

'Yeah, I managed to lose them.' Jasmine sounded amused. 'Chloe and Bethany, right?'

They nodded silently, awestruck. Not only was she talking to them, but she knew their names!

'So what happened? You've got a gorgeous voice, Bethany. I could hear you in the other songs. Then that harmony came along and you lost it totally. No way that was natural.'

Bethany took a deep breath. What should she say? It would sound so lame to admit that Lizabeth had been freaking her out.

The singer crouched down by Bethany. 'It seemed to me like that tall blonde Mary-Kate and Ashley look-alike had something to do with it. That wasn't a friendly look she was giving you.'

Bethany just nodded, relieved that she didn't have to be the one to say it.

'Lizabeth?' Chloe asked sharply. 'Bethany, why didn't you say? What's she been doing?'

Bethany shrugged. 'Oh, just being Lizabeth, I guess.'

'Don't let her get to you.' Jasmine stood up, smiling. 'Easy to say, I know. That's why I'm doing this concert, did you know that? Wish helps a lot of kids who've been bullied, and I had the worst time at school – before I went to Lane's. Tell someone next time, Bethany. Don't let her win. See you back there in a couple of minutes – you'll be fine singing it this time, I know you will.'

She was right. No one who had just been told by an Emmy award-winning singer that she had a gorgeous voice could be put off using it, even with Lizabeth still around. But Lizabeth had the look of someone who thought she might have been outsmarted, and wasn't quite sure how. She could obviously feel Bethany's new confidence.

'I'm amazed they're still letting you sing after that

little performance,' she sneered, and she looked positively furious when Bethany just smiled at her.

'Leave her alone!' Chloe's voice was a scary kind of whispered snarl to avoid the others hearing. Lizabeth had to content herself with a meaningful look at Bethany. But even that couldn't put her off now. Jasmine's praise had made the whole scholarship thing seem less important – and Chloe standing up for her made Bethany think that maybe she'd been wrong to doubt her friends. If she'd just found out she was going to film a drama series in America, *she* might not be totally on the ball with everybody else's problems either. The harmony soared above the tune, and it seemed to Bethany that she could almost feel her voice intertwining with Jasmine's. The singer gave her a thumbs up and a big smile, and Matt, the voice coach, looked delighted at the end of the song.

'Ten minutes' break certainly helped *you*,' he said, smiling at Bethany. 'Like that on the night please, everyone. Well, I think we're nearly done – Jasmine, anything else you want to run through today? Obviously we've got another rehearsal at the Albert

Hall on Thursday afternoon, and soundchecks before the concert on Friday night.'

Jasmine shook her head, smiling. 'No, it was all sounding great. Oh, one thing. I just wonder if that new song could do with something a little more? You know what I mean? I think it's got room for another voice, to give it a bit more depth. I'd like to talk to Chas about putting in a solo for Bethany on it.' She grinned at Bethany. 'You'd be all right with that, wouldn't you? You'd have time to learn it? Mr Harvey's still at Lane's isn't he – he'll just *love* teaching you a pop solo.'

Bethany giggled at the thought of Mr Harvey's face. 'I'd love it,' she said quietly.

'That's it then. See you on Thursday, everybody.' And she swept out, leaving the backing group to gather round Bethany in amazement.

Everyone got whisked off home after the rehearsal, and Bethany realised with a sudden jolt that this meant she was back at the mercy of Lizabeth – who was not a happy bunny. She simmered with rage all

the time that the school minder was taking them back on the tube, and as soon as they were alone in their bedroom she exploded.

'Just you wait, Bethany! You wait until I tell everybody what you did —'

'I didn't do anything!' Bethany protested. Jasmine and Chloe together had given her such a boost that she was starting to see Lizabeth's threats for what they really were. She still didn't want anyone to know about the scholarship – or at least, not until she'd found exactly the right moment to tell them – but she was feeling a bit more confident about her friends. 'Maybe Nadia and all your little mates would drop you if you didn't have any money, but Lily and Chloe and Sara aren't like that.' Or I don't think they are, anyway, she added to herself. 'So just shut up and leave me alone, I'm going to sleep.' And she pulled her pillow over her head to shut out any more of Lizabeth's taunts.

The next morning there was a stern reception committee waiting in the Year Seven form room.

Chloe had updated Lily and Sara on what had happened at the rehearsal and they were looking fierce.

'Why didn't you tell us?' Lily burst out, as soon as Bethany walked in the door. 'We could have helped.'

Sara was looking guilty. 'Bethany, was this what you were trying to talk to me about at break on Friday? I can't believe I let Nathan stop you telling me!'

Bethany squirmed. She still didn't want to be anybody's sympathy case, and Lizabeth's 'charity girl' comments had really got to her. She could just imagine their faces all changing when they found out. OK, she was pretty sure they wouldn't stop being her friends. But they might *feel* differently about her. Sorry for her . . . No! Of course, Lizabeth still knew, but hopefully what Bethany had said last night might have made her think she was going to tell the others about being a scholarship student anyway.

'I didn't mean not to tell you. It was just – you all had so much going on. I didn't want to spoil things. I mean, you two were so happy, and Sara – it didn't seem fair . . .' She trailed off, and then added, 'It was

just Lizabeth being Lizabeth again, after all.'

'Yes, and we know what that's like!' Lily cried. 'She's a monster. You have to tell someone, Bethany.'

Bethany frowned. 'We didn't tell anyone when she was going after you, or Sara. I'm not a baby, Lily. I can cope.'

'That's crazy. It's not about you, it's about her!' Sara put in. 'But I guess we can't make you. I should have told everybody what she did about the audition, but I was feeling so stupid that she'd taken me in.'

'Exactly.' Bethany nodded. 'I know it's stupid, but I don't want to give her the satisfaction.'

'The satisfaction of being suspended?' Lily demanded crossly.

'There's no point us having a row about it too,' Chloe said firmly. 'Anyway, Bethany, hopefully it's not going to be a problem much longer. We've got a plan. I know it's only another two nights, but you're not going back to that place with Lizabeth.'

Bethany frowned, her nose wrinkling. 'I suppose I could go back home. But then I'd have to explain why.'

'Much better plan than that.' Chloe grinned smugly. She looked so pleased with herself that Bethany was sure this was her idea. 'Come and stay with me for the next two nights. Pleeeease, Bethany! I'd love it anyway, and it gets you away from Lizabeth, and you're loads closer to school. My mum's got to get me from rehearsal anyway, so it's no extra bother for her. I'll even promise to do all my homework like an angel so I'm not distracting you!'

Bethany could feel tears pressing at the corners of her eyes. She couldn't believe that Chloe had arranged this. 'Don't your parents mind?' she asked quaveringly.

'They think it's a great idea. My mum said please come, she'd love to meet you. I've told her about Lizabeth, and she says there's no way you're going back there. She's going to call the school and sort it out, and your mum, as soon as I text her to say you're OK with it. So are you?'

Bethany nodded. 'Yes, please. Oh, yes!' And she gave Chloe a grateful hug, still trying to blink away her tears.

Chloe hugged her back excitedly. 'I can't wait. I used to have people from school round all the time, but it's harder when we all live so far away from each other. It'll be like a fab two-night sleepover!' She grabbed her phone out of her bag. 'I'll get Mum on to it straightaway.'

School felt so different that day – as though a cloud had lifted. Even when Bethany saw Lizabeth in the corridors the blonde girl's scowling face had no effect – Bethany could beam back at her without caring. She loved the thought of Lizabeth not knowing where she was at the end of the day – probably wondering if Bethany had told someone about her bullying and how she'd had to go home. Bethany hoped Lizabeth would be sweating about it all night – while she was staying with Chloe!

At the end of school Chloe was like an anxious sheepdog, herding Bethany around to grab all her stuff. Bethany had had special permission to go out at lunchtime to fetch her things from the school house, and now she had Chloe to help her carry them too. She'd had to explain a bit to Miss James

that she 'really didn't get on' with Lizabeth, and that was why she was so desperate to go home with Chloe. But she managed not to make it all sound too feeble.

'This is so cool,' Chloe bubbled, as they crammed themselves on to her train. The journey was a bit hectic, but it only took half an hour. It seemed no time to Bethany before they were walking up the path of a huge-looking house. Bethany blinked. Chloe lived here? The front door opened and Chloe's mum pattered out looking delighted. She was really like Chloe, with the same red hair and chatty friendliness.

'Bethany! I'm so glad you've come to us. Chloe's told me about that awful girl. It sounds to me as though the school really needs to deal with her, and soon.' She hustled them inside and sent them to take all Bethany's stuff upstairs while she got some snacks ready. 'We'll just have a little something now, and then dinner when Chloe's dad gets home later. You two can use the time to do your homework together, rather than Chloe doing it in front of her

TV when she's supposed to be in bed.' She gave Chloe a fake scowl, and Chloe grinned innocently back. It was lovely – Bethany really felt that Chloe's mum was as pleased as Chloe to have her there.

Chloe's room was a bit of a shock. Bethany remembered her saying something before about her mum and dad letting her use some of the money from her advert work to buy herself a DVD player – but it looked like Chloe had everything! For a start her room was enormous, with a huge bed, big wardrobes all down one side – with clothes spilling out of them all over the place – and a whole media unit with TV, computer, and all the gadgets.

'There's a sleepover bed under here,' Chloe was explaining in a muffled voice as she rooted around under her bed. 'Just have to find the right handle. There!' And she pulled a second bed out. 'Mum's put sheets and everything out for us. Do you *really* want to do your homework? I thought we could watch a DVD or something.'

Bethany considered. It did seem a waste. She fancied curling up on that comfy-looking bed – Chloe

had loads of huge fluffy cushions scattered all over it too – and watching a film.

'I've got popcorn,' Chloe added waving the bag temptingly.

'We could do that science thing while we were watching a film maybe,' Bethany said hopefully.

'Good plan. And then it's just learning that stuff for geography. We could test each other on that tomorrow when we get up, no problem. Excellent. Come on – Mum'll have got food ready for us. Do you want to change? I hate wearing my uniform at home.' Chloe flung open one of her wardrobe doors and grabbed jeans and a glittery T-shirt, and Bethany blinked at the number of clothes she had. And the shoes! *How* many pairs of trainers?

Bethany rootled through her bag for her sweat-pants, feeling out of place. There was no question – it was going to be huge fun staying with Chloe. But she so didn't want the owner of all this stuff – who apparently had no idea just how lucky she was, judging by the way she was complaining about never being able to shut her wardrobe doors – to know

what her little shared bedroom was like. It wasn't that Bethany really thought Chloe wouldn't want to be friends with her any more. That had just been Lizabeth being evil. The effort Chloe had made to help Bethany showed her that she was a real friend. But she just wasn't sure that Chloe would be able to get her head round the whole scholarship thing. And Bethany didn't fancy explaining it.

No. Her secret was just going to have to stay a secret, for the time being.

Chapter Seven

THE TRUTH COMES OUT

'Hang on girls, I need to spray your hair!' A demented-looking make-up artist was dashing around trying to make sure everyone was ready – the finishing touch was glitter hairspray to show up under the auditorium lights. She'd already managed to get Sam and Aiden, who were scowling disgustedly at their sparkly hair in the big mirrors.

'I think you should wear that to school, Sam,'

Chloe giggled. 'And baggy white trousers really suit you, Aiden. Definitely a cool new look for you.'

'If anybody'd mentioned white trousers and glitter before all this started, I'd have said no faster than the speed of light,' Sam muttered.

'Yeah, right, you were going to say no to Mr Harvey,' Aiden mocked.

'Didn't you ever have to dress up for dance shows or anything like that?' Bethany asked the boys. She'd worn more silly costumes than she could count.

Sam grinned. 'I usually managed to convince them that I wouldn't look good as a daisy or whatever it was. I was more the evil flower-eating snail type. Aaaargh! Delicious petalssssss!' He loomed over Bethany in an evil snail pose, and she and Chloe creased up.

'Glittery evil snail!' Bethany spluttered. 'I love it, Sam!'

The make-up artist scurried up. 'I haven't done you two, have I? Oh, this is going to look lovely on your hair,' she said to Bethany. She started brushing out Bethany's long black hair and spraying it

thoroughly. Bethany couldn't help gazing into the mirror. They had a couple of very simple dance moves to do during their songs, and she could tell that the glitter was going to be fabulous when she twirled around. She was pleased to find that she wasn't nervous at all – it was stupid that someone like Lizabeth could get her into such a state, but per-forming at the Albert Hall just made her feel excited.

'Are *you* nervous?' she asked Chloe curiously.

Chloe looked herself over, as though she expected to see a little sign saying yes or no. 'No, I don't think so! I think I would be if I had your solo, but I'm really jealous too.'

Bethany grinned. 'It's great though – at the moment I don't even feel nervous about that. I'm just really looking forward to it. And I'm so glad my mum and Addie are here.'

'Yeah, and Lily and Sara. It was nice of the concert people to give the school those tickets. I bet my mum can't even sit still out there right now! Ow!'

'Well, don't jump around when I'm brushing your hair,' snapped the make-up girl, and Chloe rolled her

eyes. 'You've only got a couple of minutes before you need to go into the wings, so I need to get you done.'

A runner with a headset appeared at the door. 'Everyone ready?' he asked. 'I need to take you up.'

The make-up girl released Chloe, and everyone exchanged excited looks, even Lizabeth grinning manically at Nadia and Amy. Lizabeth looked amazing, Bethany had to admit – like an ice maiden in her white trousers and vest top, with all that glittery blonde hair flying. Bethany wondered, not for the first time, if she was such good mates with Nadia because Nadia wasn't nearly as pretty as she was. That's really mean of you, Bethany Cheung, she told herself. But probably true! she added, grinning.

It was amazing, standing in the wings and watching everyone scurry around like mad bees. 'That's so-and-so, isn't it?' Chloe kept muttering in her ear, and it almost always was!

Bethany's solo part came in the last song they were singing, one that had been specially written for the concert. She had to stand with Jasmine at the front of

100

the stage. As the previous song finished, she walked slowly up to the front, telling herself firmly not to go too fast – that was the hardest thing. Bethany wasn't worried about the song, but she *was* convinced she was going to fall on her face in front of five thousand people. Jasmine beamed at her as the first notes of the song sounded, and Bethany grinned back happily. This was what she wanted to be doing for the rest of her life! Stupid stuff like Lizabeth faded into the background as Jasmine put an arm round her waist and they started to sing, the others humming and swaying gently in the background.

Was it Bethany's imagination, or could she hear Lily and Sara and Addie screaming her name out there? She scampered off the stage with the others, hardly able to believe it was over already. They crammed back into the girls' dressing room and drank Coke, all still on an adrenaline high. There was only one act after Jasmine, so it seemed just minutes later that Lily and Sara were flinging themselves into the room, followed by Chloe's parents, Bethany's mum and Addie.

'They let us come backstage,' Lily said excitedly. 'You were all brilliant. Well done! I think everyone's parents are fighting their way through Security.'

'I'm going to see if I can find my dad,' Sam said, and a few of the others followed him.

'Bethany, your solo was amazing!' Sara hugged her. 'I was so proud. I felt like nudging the people next to me and saying, I know her! She sits next to me in maths!'

Bethany's mum actually had tears in her eyes as she hugged her too. 'It was so special, Bethany, I was really proud of you. We really did make the right decision letting you apply for that scholarship. I can't believe you've done so well.'

Bethany felt all the colour and excitement draining out of her face. After all her stress about hiding the scholarship, she hadn't even *thought* to warn her mum and Addie that she hadn't told anyone. Well, how could she? It would be like saying that I think we're not good enough for Lane's, she thought to herself angrily. I've been so stupid. I should have told everyone ages ago. She looked round at Chloe,

Lily and Sara. As she'd expected, their faces were shocked, and she braced herself – she had no idea what they were going to say.

'Bethany!' yelped Sara. 'You never told us you had a scholarship!' Her eyes had darkened with surprise, and gone huge and round.

Bethany's mum looked suddenly worried, and gazed at her daughter anxiously. Bethany gripped her hand and tried to smile.

'That's so amazing,' breathed Lily. 'Do you *know* how many people were after that scholarship? Why didn't you say?'

'Still, after this evening I guess we shouldn't be surprised. When's your first album coming out, Bethany?' Chloe giggled. 'You were way better than Jasmine.'

Bethany's lungs stopped feeling as though they'd broken, and she took in a deep breath. 'I just never found a good moment to tell you. Um, sorry . . .'

Sara shook her head. 'Why are you apologising, silly? It's not one of those things you go round telling everybody, is it? "Hi, I'm Bethany and I'm so

outstandingly brilliant that Lane's gave me a scholarship."'

'We'd all have kicked you,' Chloe said, grinning. 'Actually, can I kick you now? Just to make sure you don't get too full of yourself.'

Addie, who'd been perching next to Bethany against the dressing table, suddenly gulped and nodded towards the door. 'Look,' she whispered excitedly.

It was Jasmine, looking amazing still in her stage costume, her face flushed with the excitement of the performance.

'Oh wow,' Addie muttered, star-struck.

Jasmine smiled at everyone, and then homed in on Bethany. 'I just wanted to come and say well done.' She grinned. 'And also ask if you're busy early on next year, 'cause I'm recording the new album, and I really like your voice. I'd like you to sing with me on a couple of tracks.'

Bethany could feel Addie trembling with excitement next to her.

'Yes!' Bethany squeaked, her voice disappearing

entirely. Over Jasmine's shoulder she caught sight of Lizabeth, frozen to the spot with horror. The scary, worried feeling that had been lurking inside her for the last couple of weeks suddenly disappeared, and she beamed at Jasmine. 'Oh, yes, please!'

Enjoy the other BRILLIANT and

fun-filled adventures in the

STAGE
School series!

Chloe was used to being the star of the class in her old school – always the funniest, brightest and most extrovert. But the *Marcia Lane School of Drama and Dance* is different. This isn't a place for showing off. All the pupils are stars in their own way. Will Chloe learn that acting the fool and being a good actress are not the same thing?

Sara is desperate to perform well in her audition for a leading role in **Mary Poppins**, but Lizabeth, another talented student, has her eye on the same role and she is prepared to go to extremes to make sure the part is hers. Can Sara keep her cool and shine like a star?

Lily is used to pressure. Her mother is a famous actress and has always wanted Lily to follow in her footsteps. But Lily doesn't really want to be an actress – she wants to be herself. Then one day she gets the chance to audition for a fantastic part and she has to decide what she really wants. Is it too late to change her mind? Is there still time for her to become a STAR?

Bethany finds being a scholarship girl at the *Marcia Lane School of Drama and Dance* isn't that easy. Her long journey to school and the endless homework are hard enough, but on top of that she is trying to keep her scholarship secret. Then she gets the chance to perform in an exciting charity concert with world-famous Jasmine Day. But can Bethany cope with school and live her dream?

STAGE
School
Where Dreams Are Made!

'I'll help you and you'll help me,
For we are Sisters of the Sea!'

Look out for the new Arctica Mermaids series coming soon . . .

To order any of these titles direct from
Bloomsbury Publishing visit
www.bloomsbury.com/bookshop
or call 020 7440 2475